# The Haunter of the Dark

*Lovecraft's Tale of Cosmic Horror –*
*Ancient Evil Awakens*

## A Modern Translation

Adapted for the Contemporary Reader

## H.P. Lovecraft

Translated by Tim Zengerink

# Table of Contents

# Preface - Message to the Reader

### What If You Could Help Rebuild the Greatest Library in Human History?

Thousands of years ago, the Library of Alexandria stood as the crown jewel of human achievement — a sanctuary where the collected wisdom of every known civilization was gathered, preserved, and shared freely.

And then, it was lost.

Through fire, conquest, and the slow erosion of time, humanity lost not just books — but ideas, dreams, discoveries, and stories that could have changed the world forever.

Today, the Library of Alexandria lives again — and you are invited to be a part of its restoration.

Our mission is simple yet profound:

To rebuild the greatest library the world has ever known, and to translate all timeless works into every language and dialect, so that no seeker of knowledge is ever left behind again.

By joining our movement to rebuild the modern Library of Alexandria, you become part of an unprecedented mission:

- **Unlimited Access to the Greatest Audiobooks & eBooks Ever Written:**

  Instantly explore thousands of legendary works—Plato, Shakespeare, Jane Austen, Leo Tolstoy, and countless more. All instantly available to read or listen, placing a complete literary universe at your fingertips.

- **Beautiful Paperback & Deluxe Editions at Printing Cost**

  Own any title as an elegant paperback, deluxe hardcover, or stunning collectible boxset—offered to you at true printing cost, delivered straight to your door. Build your personal Library of Alexandria, crafted for beauty, built for durability, and worthy of proud display.

- **Fresh Translations for Modern Readers—in Every Language & Dialect**

  Enjoy timeless masterpieces reimagined in clear, contemporary language—no more outdated phrases or obscure references. Alongside the original versions, we're tirelessly translating these classics into every language and dialect imaginable, ensuring accessibility and understanding across cultures and generations.

- **Join a Global Renaissance of Literature & Knowledge**

  You directly support expanding our library, publishing deluxe editions at true cost, translating works into all global languages, and bringing humanity's greatest stories to people everywhere. By joining today, you're not just preserving a legacy of masterpieces; you set in motion a powerful wave of literary accessibility.

**Become a Torchbearer of Knowledge.**

Join us for free now at **LibraryofAlexandria.com**

Together, we will ensure that the light of human wisdom never fades again.

With gratitude and a shared love of knowledge,

The Modern Library of Alexandria Team

Visit:

www.libraryofalexandria.com

Or scan the code below:

# Introduction

## Forbidden Curiosity, Urban Shadows, and the Price of Seeing

H.P. Lovecraft's "The Haunter of the Dark," written in 1935 and published posthumously in Weird Tales in December 1936, is a masterwork of psychological and metaphysical horror. It serves as a spiritual sequel to his earlier tale, "The Shambler from the Stars," written by fellow horror writer Robert Bloch, and completes a dark, intertextual dialogue between the two. In this narrative, Lovecraft returns to a familiar theme: the dire consequences of seeking knowledge that is not meant to be known. But unlike many of his earlier tales, which take place in rural settings or distant epochs, "The Haunter of the Dark" is rooted in a deeply urban landscape—Providence's fictionalized twin, set against the gothic skyline of Federal Hill in Rhode Island. It's an ominous reminder that the veil between the known and the unknowable is thin even in the heart of civilization.

The story follows Robert Blake, a young writer and artist with an affinity for the arcane, who becomes fascinated by a brooding, long-abandoned church visible from his apartment window. Moved by both his artistic sensibilities and his morbid curiosity, he investigates the building, only to discover that it was once home to a mysterious and heretical sect known as the Church of Starry Wisdom. Their worship centered around a strange artifact—the Shining Trapezohedron—a window into other dimensions and the source of communication with an ancient and malevolent being: the Haunter of the Dark.

Blake's investigation leads him deeper into madness and spiritual peril. He learns that the church has a history of disappearances and madness, and that the entity they summoned can only manifest in darkness. Once Blake physically visits the church and gazes into the Trapezohedron, he becomes marked—watched, haunted, and eventually hunted by the being he has awakened. The story culminates in a citywide blackout during a thunderstorm, when the Haunter is finally able to breach the bounds of its imprisonment. Blake's final moments are recorded only through his last journal entries, recovered after his death—an ending as chilling as it is inevitable.

"The Haunter of the Dark" reflects a more mature Lovecraft. By 1935, his style had evolved into something leaner and more deliberate. Gone are the overabundant adjectives and florid descriptors of his earlier work. What remains is dread—carefully built, surgically deployed, and devastating in its restraint. The story is told through indirect testimony, third-person distance, and recovered documents—techniques Lovecraft used masterfully to suggest rather than show, to hint rather than explain. And through these suggestions, he conveys the horror of cosmic insignificance and spiritual annihilation more potently than ever.

The Haunter itself, a creature of blasphemous ambiguity, is never fully seen. It is described only in fragments—as a shadow with wings, a presence in the dark, an entity linked with ancient stars and forgotten rituals. Its mystery is its menace. It belongs to Lovecraft's pantheon of Great Old Ones, but even more so than Cthulhu or Nyarlathotep, it resists classification. It is unknowable, unstoppable, and inimical to life. And yet it is summoned not by evil intention, but by curiosity—a hallmark of Lovecraft's most enduring theme: that the pursuit of knowledge beyond human comprehension leads not to revelation, but to ruin.

# The Church of Starry Wisdom, Cosmic Terror, and Lovecraft's Final Word

Lovecraft's choice to set the story in a decaying urban church is not accidental. The Church of Starry Wisdom, with its esoteric rituals, cryptic history, and sinister relics, stands as a symbol of the corruption of traditional belief systems. It represents the collapse of spiritual meaning in the face of a greater, darker reality. The sect is not portrayed as evil in the conventional sense—they are seekers, mystics, visionaries. But in their attempt to commune with the cosmos, they instead touch something ancient and alien—something that cannot be understood, bargained with, or exorcised. In this way, Lovecraft critiques both science and religion, suggesting that neither is equipped to confront the reality that lies beyond the stars.

Robert Blake serves as a surrogate for Lovecraft himself. A writer, artist, dreamer, and philosopher, Blake is driven by aesthetic fascination as much as by intellectual ambition. He is drawn to the church not merely to investigate its secrets, but to experience its mood, its symbolism, its presence. He writes about it, sketches it, dreams about it. In this, Lovecraft inserts his own sensibilities into the narrative—the belief that beauty and terror are entwined, that to truly appreciate the sublime is to court madness. Blake is not a hero. He is not brave. He is a man who looks too long at something no one should ever see, and he pays the price.

The Shining Trapezohedron, the glowing relic at the heart of the church's unholy rites, is more than a mystical object. It is a narrative device—a literal and metaphorical window. Through it, Blake sees into other dimensions, glimpses alien geometries, and senses the presence of the Haunter. But he also sees himself. His fate is tied to the act of vision. He looks, and in looking, he is undone. The Trapezohedron reflects not just external horrors, but internal truths. It reveals to Blake—and to us—that the universe is not anthropocentric, not moral, not comprehensible. It is a cold, indifferent expanse, filled with entities and energies that exist beyond our capacity for understanding.

And yet, there is tragedy here. "The Haunter of the Dark" is not a story of punishment, but of inevitability. Blake is not damned by vice, but by vision. He represents the modern man, armed with intellect and imagination, seeking truth in a universe that has no obligation to reveal itself. His death is not a moral lesson—it is an existential certainty. Lovecraft does not judge Blake. He pities him. In Blake's fall, Lovecraft encapsulates the human condition: to seek, to reach, to look—and to find that the darkness looks back.

Written near the end of Lovecraft's life, this story feels like a culmination. It contains within it the DNA of his entire oeuvre: the lost sects of "The Dunwich Horror," the alien geometry of "The Dreams in the Witch House," the unseen dread of "The Colour Out of Space," and the madness-inducing relics of "The Call of Cthulhu." But here, these elements are streamlined, sharpened, and rendered with masterful control. This is Lovecraft at the height of his abilities, delivering a story that is both compact and expansive, intimate and cosmic, grounded and terrifyingly unmoored.

This modern edition of "The Haunter of the Dark" retains the structure, tone, and philosophical weight of the original while refining archaic language and syntax for the contemporary reader. Every sentence has been evaluated for clarity and resonance, ensuring that Lovecraft's vision is not only preserved but illuminated. The terror remains untouched. The shadows remain deep. The church still stands, waiting.

To enter "The Haunter of the Dark" is to engage with the idea that the world we inhabit is only a thin layer of comfort stretched over a chasm of unknown depth. It is to follow a man who seeks beauty in darkness and finds only oblivion. It is to learn that some places should not be visited, some truths should not be uncovered, and some lights—like the Trapezohedron—do not reveal, but erase. The story offers no closure, no explanation, no redemption. Only the echo of wings in the dark, and the knowledge that something vast, ancient, and watchful waits just beyond the reach of our fragile lights.

Dedicated to Robert Bloch

# The Haunter of the Dark

I've seen the universe open wide in darkness,
Where black planets drift with no direction—
They move in silence, full of fear,
Unknown, unseen, and without any light or name.

—Nemesis.

Careful researchers might hesitate to go against the popular belief that Robert Blake died from a lightning strike, or maybe from a powerful shock caused by electricity. The window he had been looking out of wasn't broken, but nature can behave in strange ways. The look on his face could've come from something simple, like a muscle spasm, and his diary entries seem clearly inspired by an overactive imagination fueled by local legends and the strange old stories he'd been investigating. As for the strange things that happened at the empty church on Federal Hill, many logical thinkers blame them on some kind of trick or prank—perhaps even one Blake was secretly involved in.

After all, Blake was a writer and artist who focused entirely on myths, dreams, horror, and the supernatural. He loved looking for weird places and spooky atmospheres. During a previous stay in the city, he had visited an unusual old man obsessed with the same dark topics, and that trip had ended in a mysterious fire and death. It's possible something deep inside him drew him back from Milwaukee, even if he claimed in his diary not to know about the local legends. Some believe his death may have stopped what could've been an elaborate hoax that he had planned to turn into a story.

Still, there are some who believe a more unusual explanation. These people take Blake's diary seriously and point to strange facts: the church records were proven real, the strange religious group known as the Starry Wisdom sect did exist before 1877, a curious journalist named Edwin M. Lillibridge really did vanish in 1893, and most of all—Blake's face when he died was frozen in overwhelming terror. One of these believers, deeply convinced and a little extreme, threw a strange stone and metal box into the bay. These objects had been found in the dark steeple of the church—not the tower where Blake's diary said they were. Though he was criticized for it, this man, a respected doctor with a love for odd legends, claimed he had destroyed something too dangerous to remain in the world.

Now, between these two sides—those who doubt and those who believe—the reader must decide. The newspapers shared the facts with a skeptical tone, leaving it up to others to imagine what Robert Blake saw... or thought he saw... or maybe just pretended to see.

If we take a step back and carefully look at his diary, we can try to piece together the chilling chain of events from Blake's point of view.

He returned to Providence in the winter of 1934-35, moving into the top floor of an old house on a quiet, grassy court off College Street. It sat on the crest of a hill near Brown University and behind the marble John Hay Library. It was a cozy, charming spot in a tiny garden oasis surrounded by old buildings, where big friendly cats liked to stretch out in the sun on a nearby shed. The house was an old Georgian-style building with a classic doorway, small-paned windows, and other touches from the early 1800s. Inside, it had old wooden floors, a curving staircase, and elegant fireplace mantels. The back rooms were set slightly lower than the rest of the house.

Blake used a large room on the southwest side as his study. One side looked out over the front garden, while the west-facing windows—where he placed his desk— gave him an incredible view of the city's rooftops below and the glowing sunsets behind them. Far off in the distance, he could see the rolling purple hills of the countryside. About two miles away stood the ghostly rise of Federal Hill, packed with rooftops and spires that seemed to shift and take strange shapes as the city's smoke swirled around them. Sometimes, Blake felt as though he was looking at a dreamy, otherworldly place—one that might vanish like a dream if he ever tried to visit it in real life.

Blake had most of his books sent from home, bought some antique furniture to match the style of his new place, and settled into a quiet routine of writing and painting. He lived alone and took care of the house himself. His art studio was in an upstairs attic room with a special roof that let in a lot of natural light. That winter, he wrote five of his most well-known short stories— The Burrower Beneath, The Stairs in the Crypt, Shaggai, In the Vale of Pnath, and The Feaster from the Stars. He also painted seven pieces, most of them showing strange, unearthly monsters and alien landscapes from other worlds.

At sunset, Blake often sat at his desk and stared dreamily out toward the west. He could see Memorial Hall's dark towers below, the old courthouse's bell tower, the tall buildings downtown, and, far in the distance, the shining hill covered in rooftops and steeples. This mysterious hill, with its twisted streets and maze-like houses, stirred his imagination. From the few people he knew in town, he learned that the distant hill was a large Italian neighborhood, though many of the houses were older and came from earlier times when Yankees and Irish families lived there. Sometimes, Blake used binoculars to study the faraway hill. He would look closely at the rooftops, chimneys, and church spires, imagining all kinds of strange and magical secrets they might hide. Even with the help of the binoculars, Federal Hill still seemed far away and dreamlike, as if it belonged in one of the weird stories or paintings Blake created. That feeling lingered long after the sun had set, when the hill faded into the purple twilight and the courthouse lights and the glowing red beacon from the Industrial Trust Building lit up the night in an eerie way.

Of all the things he could see on Federal Hill, one huge, dark church stood out most to Blake. It caught his attention at certain times of day, especially at sunset when its tall tower and narrow steeple looked like a black shadow against the fiery sky. It seemed to be built on one of the highest points of the hill. Its dirty stone front and steep roof, with tall pointed windows just visible on the north side, rose sharply above the surrounding buildings. The church looked old and serious, its stones stained by years of smoke and rain. Its style seemed to be an early version of Gothic revival architecture—something older and less polished than later designs. Blake guessed it was built around 1810 or 1815.

As time went on, Blake's fascination with the creepy, distant church grew stronger. Since he never saw any lights in its huge windows, he was sure it was abandoned. The more he stared at it, the more his imagination wandered. Eventually, he convinced himself that the church had a strange feeling of loneliness or decay about it—something so heavy and strange that even birds stayed away. He noticed how pigeons and swallows gathered on other rooftops and towers, but never on this one. At least, that's what he believed, and it's what he wrote in his diary. He pointed the church out to some of his friends, but none of them had ever been to Federal Hill or had any idea what the building was or used to be.

When spring came, Blake began to feel very unsettled. He had started writing a novel he had been planning for a long time—about an old witch-cult that had survived in Maine—but he couldn't seem to make any progress. He found himself spending more and more time just sitting at his window, staring at the distant hill and the dark church that the birds seemed to avoid. Even though the garden outside was now full of blooming trees and bright colors, Blake's unease only got worse. That's when he first began thinking about actually crossing the city and climbing that far-off hill to see the mysterious, smoke-covered world for himself.

In late April, just before the old, mysterious time of Walpurgis, Blake finally decided to visit the strange place he had only seen from afar. He walked through busy downtown streets and run-down old neighborhoods until he reached a steep street lined with worn-out steps, sagging porches, and dusty windows. It felt like he was getting close to that distant, hidden world he had always wondered about. The street signs didn't mean anything to him, and the people around him had unfamiliar, dark faces. The shops had foreign writing, and the buildings were old and weathered. He couldn't find any of the landmarks he had seen through his binoculars, and for a moment, he thought maybe Federal Hill had only been a dream.

Every so often he would spot an old church or tower, but never the dark one he was looking for. When he asked a shop owner about a large stone church, the man just smiled and shook his head, even though he spoke English. As Blake climbed higher, the area seemed even stranger. Narrow alleys stretched out in confusing directions, and nothing looked familiar. He crossed a few large streets and thought he saw a tower he recognized. When he asked another shopkeeper about the church, the man pretended not to know—but Blake could tell he was lying. The man looked scared and made a strange hand sign.

Then, out of nowhere, Blake saw the tall black spire rising into the sky. It stood above the brown rooftops to the south. He knew instantly that it was the church he had been searching for. He rushed toward it through the muddy backstreets, losing his way a couple of times. But he felt nervous about asking anyone for help—not the old men or women sitting on their steps, or even the kids playing in the dirt.

Finally, he reached a wide, open square with cobblestones and a tall wall on the far side. He knew his search was over. On a raised area, about six feet above the rest of the square and surrounded by an iron fence, stood the huge, dark church he had seen so many times from a distance.

The church was falling apart. Some of the stone supports had collapsed, and broken decorations lay hidden in the overgrown weeds. The dark, dirty windows were mostly still in place, though parts of the frames were missing. Blake was surprised that the stained glass hadn't been shattered by kids. The heavy doors were shut tight. The rusty fence around the churchyard was locked, and the path to the entrance was completely covered in grass and vines. The whole place felt empty and forgotten. The silence, the crumbling stone, and the lifeless walls gave off a creepy feeling that Blake couldn't explain.

There weren't many people in the square, but Blake spotted a police officer nearby and went over to ask about the church. The officer was a big Irishman, and Blake thought it was strange when he simply made the sign of the cross and said that people didn't talk about that place. When Blake pushed for more information, the man quickly added that the local Italian priests warned everyone to stay away. They believed something evil had once lived there and had left behind a curse. The officer also said his father used to speak in whispers about strange sounds and rumors from his own childhood.

There had once been a dangerous group in that church long ago—a group that was said to call up terrible things from some dark, unknown place. It took a strong priest to drive out whatever they had summoned, though some people said that just shining a light could have done it. If Father O'Malley were still alive, he could tell many stories about what had happened. But now, there was nothing to do but leave the place alone. It didn't hurt anyone anymore, and the people who had once owned it were either dead or long gone. They had left like rats after the rumors in 1877, when neighbors started noticing how people sometimes vanished without a trace. Someday the city would probably take over the building since no one had claimed it, but messing with it wouldn't do any good. It was better to let it fall apart over time—some things should stay buried in the dark forever.

After the policeman left, Blake stood staring at the gloomy, steepled church. He felt oddly thrilled to know others found the building just as eerie as he did, and he began to wonder if there was any truth in the old stories the officer had told him. Maybe the tales were just superstitions inspired by the church's creepy look—but even then, they felt like something out of one of his own horror stories.

The afternoon sun peeked out from the clouds, but it still couldn't brighten the stained, grimy walls of the church. It was strange how none of the fresh spring green had touched the dead plants growing in the fenced-in yard. Blake found himself stepping closer, inspecting the wall and rusted iron fence for a way in. There was something about the dark, ruined building that drew him in, no matter how unsettling it felt. The front gate by the steps was locked, but on the north side, some of the bars were missing. He could walk along the narrow ledge around the fence and slip through the gap.

If people were truly that afraid of the place, no one would stop him.

He climbed up the embankment and had nearly made it inside before anyone noticed. Then, when he glanced back down, he saw the few people in the square slowly backing away, making the same strange hand sign the shopkeeper had made. Several windows slammed shut, and a heavyset woman rushed into the street to pull a few children inside a worn-down house. Blake passed through the gap in the fence easily and found himself walking through the overgrown, rotting weeds of the abandoned yard. Here and there, the broken base of an old headstone showed that this had once been a graveyard—but that must have been many years ago. Up close, the size of the church felt even more overwhelming, but Blake pushed past his fear and stepped toward the three large front doors. They were all locked tight, so he began circling the massive building, looking for a smaller door or window he could get through. Even though part of him wasn't sure he wanted to go inside, something about the church kept pulling him closer.

Eventually, he found an open, broken basement window in the back. Leaning in, Blake saw a dark, cobweb-filled space below, dimly lit by the last light of the day. He could see old barrels, broken furniture, and scattered junk, all covered in a thick layer of dust that blurred their shapes. A rusted furnace showed that the church had still been in use at least through the mid-1800s.

Without really thinking, Blake climbed through the basement window and dropped down onto the dusty, cluttered concrete floor. The basement was huge and open, with no walls dividing it. In a dark corner to the right, he spotted a black archway that seemed to lead upstairs. Being inside the eerie old building made him feel uneasy, but he stayed calm and began looking around. He found a barrel that was still intact and rolled it over to the window to use later as a step to climb back out. Then, gathering his courage, he moved across the dusty, cobweb-covered floor toward the archway. Dust filled the air and stuck to him like a thick film, but he kept going. He climbed the old stone steps in the dark, feeling his way with his hands. After turning a corner, he reached a door. He fumbled for the latch and finally managed to open it. On the other side was a dim hallway with rotting wooden paneling.

Now on the main floor, Blake moved quickly from room to room, finding that all the doors inside were unlocked. The giant central room—the nave—was a haunting sight. Thick dust covered everything: the pews, the altar, the pulpit, even the hourglass and sounding board. Enormous spiderwebs hung between the pointed arches and wrapped around the tall Gothic columns. A gloomy, grayish light came through the stained glass windows as the afternoon sun slipped lower in the sky.

The stained glass was so covered in soot that Blake could barely see the images. From what little he could make out, he didn't like them. Most were symbolic designs, and his knowledge of ancient symbols told him they were strange and unsettling. The saints shown in the windows had odd, unpleasant expressions. One window showed nothing but a dark space with swirling lights scattered across it. When he turned away from the windows, he noticed something odd about the cross above the altar—it wasn't the usual shape. Instead, it looked like the ancient Egyptian ankh.

In a small room near the back, next to the apse, Blake found a rotting desk and tall shelves packed with moldy, falling-apart books. This was the first time he felt real fear, because the books were ones he recognized—books filled with forbidden and dangerous knowledge. These were titles that most people had never even heard of, or only whispered about in secret: banned books full of ancient secrets passed down through time from before humanity even existed. Blake had read some of them before—books like the Latin Necronomicon, Liber Ivonis, Cultes des Goules by Comte d'Erlette, Unaussprechlichen Kulten by von Junzt, and De Vermis Mysteriis by Ludvig Prinn. But there were others he only knew by name—or not at all—like the Pnakotic Manuscripts, the Book of Dzyan, and a crumbling book written in symbols he couldn't recognize, though some of the strange signs and diagrams were chillingly familiar to anyone who studied the occult.

Clearly, the old stories were true. This church had once been a center of dark, ancient evil—something older than mankind and bigger than anything we know.

Inside the broken desk, Blake found a small leather book filled with handwritten entries in a secret code. The writing used traditional symbols from astronomy, alchemy, and astrology—things like the sun, moon, planets, zodiac signs, and more—all packed together in strange patterns. The layout of the text suggested that each symbol might stand for a letter of the alphabet.

Hoping to decode it later, Blake tucked the small book into his coat pocket. Many of the big old books on the shelves drew him in, and he thought he might return later to borrow some. He couldn't believe they had sat untouched for so long. Had he really been the first to fight past the thick, overwhelming fear that had kept this place empty for nearly sixty years?

Blake had finished exploring the ground floor and made his way back through the dusty main hall to the front entrance. There, he had noticed a staircase leading up into the dark tower and steeple—landmarks he'd long observed from a distance. Climbing up was difficult, as the air was thick with dust and cobwebs covered everything. The stairs spiraled tightly upward, with narrow wooden steps, and now and then he passed foggy windows that gave dizzying views of the city below. He had expected to find a bell or set of bells up in the tower—especially after seeing the steeple so often through his field glasses—but he was surprised and disappointed to find that the top chamber was completely empty of any chimes. Instead, it was clearly used for something else.

The small room, about fifteen feet wide, was dimly lit by four tall, narrow windows—one on each wall. These windows were partly covered with decaying wooden shutters and old, cracked screens, now mostly falling apart. In the middle of the dusty floor stood a strange stone pillar, about four feet high and two feet wide. It was carved with bizarre, rough symbols that Blake couldn't recognize. On top of the pillar sat a metal box with an odd, lopsided shape. Its lid was open, and inside—under a thick layer of dust—was what looked like a round or egg-shaped object, about four inches across.

Around the pillar were seven tall, Gothic-style chairs, most of them still in good condition. Behind the chairs, along the walls, stood seven huge statues made of black-painted plaster. They were cracked and worn, and looked eerily like the mysterious stone heads found on Easter Island. In one corner of the room, a wooden ladder was built into the wall. It led up to a trapdoor that opened into the steeple above, which had no windows.

As Blake's eyes adjusted to the dim light, he took a closer look at the strange box. He brushed away the dust and saw disturbing carvings on its sides—alien shapes that seemed alive but didn't look like anything that could exist on Earth. The round object in the box wasn't perfectly smooth. It was a dark stone, streaked with red, and shaped like a many-sided crystal. It might have been a rare gem or something man-made, carefully carved and polished. It didn't rest at the bottom of the box; instead, a metal band around its middle held it up, supported by seven small arms that connected to the box's top edges.

As soon as the stone was fully visible, Blake felt strangely drawn to it. He couldn't stop staring. Its shiny surfaces almost seemed see-through, as if he could see entire worlds inside it. His mind filled with strange images—distant planets with towering stone buildings, barren alien landscapes with enormous mountains, and far-off places where something moved silently in the dark, just enough to hint at a hidden awareness.

When Blake finally looked away, his eyes were drawn to a strange-looking pile of dust in the far corner, near the ladder. He couldn't explain why it caught his attention, but something about its shape made him uneasy. He walked toward it, pushing through cobwebs, and began brushing the dust away. What he uncovered shocked him—it was a human skeleton that had clearly been there for a very long time. The clothes had almost completely rotted away, but some old buttons and fabric scraps showed that it had once been a man in a gray suit.

There were more clues—worn-out shoes, broken metal fasteners, large cuff buttons, an old-fashioned stickpin, and a reporter's badge that read Providence Telegram. Nearby was a crumbling leather wallet. Blake carefully opened it and found old paper money, a small plastic calendar from 1893, some calling cards with the name Edwin M. Lillibridge, and a piece of paper covered with handwritten notes in pencil.

The paper was full of strange and confusing notes, and Blake read through it carefully by the dim light of the west-facing window. The writing was scattered and disjointed, but included lines like:

"Prof. Enoch Bowen comes back from Egypt in May 1844—buys old Free-Will Church in July—his archaeology and occult studies are well known."

"Dr. Drowne of the 4th Baptist Church warns about Starry Wisdom in his sermon on December 29, 1844."

"97 members in the congregation by the end of 1845."

"1846—3 people go missing—first time the Shining Trapezohedron is mentioned."

"7 more disappearances in 1848—rumors of blood sacrifices begin."

"An investigation in 1853 leads nowhere—people talk about strange sounds."

"Father O'Malley tells of devil worship linked to a box found in ancient Egyptian ruins—says it calls up something that can't survive in the light. It fears light and gets banished by strong light. Then it has to be summoned again. He probably heard this from the deathbed confession of Francis X. Feeney, who joined Starry Wisdom in 1849. Members claim the Shining Trapezohedron shows them heaven and other worlds, and that the 'Haunter of the Dark' reveals secrets to them."

"Orrin B. Eddy story in 1857. They stare into the crystal to call it, and have their own secret language."

"Over 200 members in 1863, not counting men fighting in the war."

"Irish boys riot at the church in 1869 after Patrick Regan disappears."

"A vague newspaper article appears March 14, 1872, but people don't discuss it."

"6 more disappearances in 1876—a secret committee meets with Mayor Doyle."

"Action is promised in February 1877—the church closes in April."

"A gang—Federal Hill Boys—threaten the pastor and church staff in May."

"181 people leave the city before the end of 1877—no names are mentioned."

"Ghost stories begin around 1880—try to confirm the claim that no person has entered the church since 1877."

"Ask Lanigan for a photo of the place taken in 1851..."

Blake folded the paper, placed it back into the wallet, and tucked the wallet into his coat. Then he looked down at the skeleton lying in the dust. The notes made it clear what had happened: the man must have come to the abandoned church forty-two years earlier to chase a news story no one else had dared to pursue. Maybe no one even knew he planned to come here. But he had never returned. Had something terrified him so badly that it caused a sudden heart attack?

Blake crouched to examine the bones more closely. Some were scattered, and a few looked strangely melted at the ends. Others had turned an odd yellow color, with signs of being slightly burned. Even pieces of the clothing had burn marks. The skull was especially strange—yellowed with a burned hole at the top, like it had been eaten away by a strong acid. Blake had no idea what could've happened to the body during those forty silent years.

He had come to the empty building hoping to find a story exciting enough for the newspaper.

Before he realized it, Blake found himself staring at the stone again, letting its strange power fill his mind with strange and hazy visions. He imagined long lines of hooded figures that didn't look human and endless deserts filled with tall, carved stones reaching into the sky. He saw towers and walls deep under the ocean and swirling areas in space where black mist floated in front of faint purple glows. Beyond everything, he imagined a vast space of total darkness, where strange shapes moved and invisible forces seemed to bring order to chaos—offering answers to the mysteries of the universe.

Suddenly, the spell broke. A wave of fear hit him— vague, but strong. Blake gasped and looked away from the stone, feeling like something was near him— something not from the stone itself, but something that had looked through it at him. It wasn't watching with eyes, but with a presence that Blake could feel. He sensed he had stirred something that would now always follow him. He told himself it was just nerves, which wasn't surprising after what he'd just seen. The light was fading, too, and since he had brought no flashlight, he knew it was time to leave.

As the light dimmed, he thought he saw a faint glow coming from the strange, oddly-shaped stone. Even though he tried to look away, something deep inside him made him look back. Was the stone slightly glowing because of radiation? He remembered what the dead man's notes had said about the Shining Trapezohedron. What kind of evil place had he stumbled into? What had once happened here—and what might still be hiding in the dark shadows where no birds flew?

He thought he smelled something faint and foul nearby, though he couldn't tell where it came from. Quickly, he shut the lid of the strange metal box holding the glowing stone. It closed easily with a sharp click.

Just as it shut, a soft sound came from above in the pitch-black steeple. It had to be rats—the only living things he'd seen or heard since arriving. But the noise frightened him more than it should have. He ran down the spiral staircase, across the dusty main room, through the basement, out into the dark square, and down the eerie streets and alleys of Federal Hill. He didn't stop until he was back in the well-lit, familiar part of the city near the college.

In the days that followed, Blake didn't tell anyone where he had gone. Instead, he spent his time reading strange old books, digging through years of old newspapers, and trying to solve the code in the leather notebook he had taken from the church. The writing was tricky. After a lot of work, he figured out that the language wasn't English, Latin, or any common tongue. It seemed ancient, and Blake realized he would need to dig deep into his strange knowledge to understand it.

Each night, he still felt the urge to look out toward the west, where he could see the black steeple among the city rooftops. But now, what once felt mysterious now filled him with dread. He knew now what kind of ancient, dark knowledge the tower held, and his imagination raced with eerie new thoughts. As the spring birds returned, Blake noticed they avoided the tall, lonely spire more than ever. When they got near, they turned sharply and scattered, as if something scared them. Though he couldn't hear their cries, he could picture their panic.

By June, Blake's diary said he had finally cracked the code. The writing turned out to be in the ancient Aklo language—used by evil cults in the distant past. Blake only knew a little of it from his previous studies. He didn't write down much of what he found, but what he did say made it clear that what he discovered scared him. He wrote about a being called the Haunter of the Dark, which was awakened by looking into the glowing crystal. The being knew everything, but it demanded terrible sacrifices. Blake feared that the creature had been awakened and could now roam free—though he also believed that it couldn't cross into the light of the street lamps.

Blake wrote about the Shining Trapezohedron often. He called it a window to all time and space and said it had a long, dark history. It had been created on a distant world called Yuggoth, long before alien beings brought it to Earth. It had passed through many hands: hidden by strange creatures in Antarctica, then taken by serpent-men, then studied by the first humans in Lemuria. It had sunk with Atlantis, been found by a fisherman, and later sold to merchants from ancient Egypt. The Pharaoh Nephren-Ka built a temple around it—but did such terrible things with it that his name was erased from all records. The temple was later destroyed, but the glowing stone was buried and hidden—until it was uncovered again, ready to bring misfortune to humankind.

In July, the newspapers quietly reported things that matched what Blake wrote in his diary. People in Federal Hill had grown uneasy since someone entered the old church. The locals whispered about strange sounds coming from the steeple—bumping, scraping, and stirring. They had nightmares and begged their priests to banish whatever spirit haunted the place. Something, they said, was waiting behind a door, checking to see if it was dark enough to come out.

The newspapers didn't go into detail, but Blake's diary did. He wrote with regret, feeling guilty for uncovering the glowing stone and possibly waking the evil being. He felt it was his duty to bury the stone and let light into the steeple to drive the creature away. Still, he couldn't deny his obsession. Even in his dreams, he longed to return to that cursed tower and stare once more into the glowing crystal that showed him things beyond human understanding.

Then something Blake read in the morning paper on July 17 filled him with fear. It was just another one of those strange and slightly funny reports about people on Federal Hill being nervous, but to Blake, it felt deeply serious. A thunderstorm had knocked out the city's power for an hour the night before, and during that dark time, the people living near the old church were terrified. They swore that something inside the steeple had taken advantage of the darkness and moved down into the main part of the church, making awful flopping and thumping sounds. Near the end of the blackout, they heard crashing sounds from the tower, as if glass had shattered. They said this thing could only move in total darkness, and even a little bit of light would send it running.

When the power finally came back on, there was a loud noise in the tower. Even the small amount of light filtering through the dirty, boarded-up windows had been too much for the creature. It had rushed back up to the black steeple just in time—because if it had stayed in the light too long, it might have been banished back to wherever it came from. During that dark hour, people had gathered outside the church, holding candles and lamps hidden under paper and umbrellas to keep them lit. They were trying to protect the city with light. Some people closest to the church even said the outer door had rattled during the storm.

But that wasn't the worst part. Later that evening, Blake read more in the Bulletin. A couple of reporters, finally taking the strange events seriously, had slipped into the church through the cellar window after finding the doors locked. Inside, they saw the dust disturbed in strange ways, and the cushions and fabric from the pews were torn and scattered. The air smelled terrible, and there were yellow stains and patches that looked burnt. When they opened the door to the tower, they thought they heard something scrape above them. The narrow stairs had been roughly swept clean, as if something had moved through.

Up in the tower, they found the same strange signs: the stone pedestal with its odd shape, the fallen Gothic chairs, and the huge cracked statues along the wall. But they didn't mention the metal box or the skeleton that

Blake had found. What bothered Blake most was the broken glass. All the tower's tall windows were shattered, and in two of them, someone had stuffed in fabric and horsehair, like they were trying to block out the light again. More of the same materials were scattered on the floor, as if whoever was doing this had been interrupted.

There were also yellow stains and burn marks on the ladder leading to the top steeple. One reporter had climbed it, opened the trapdoor, and shined a flashlight into the pitch black space—but saw nothing except broken pieces lying around. People said it was all a trick. Some thought someone had faked the whole thing to scare the locals. Others believed it was a prank by the younger crowd. The police eventually sent someone to check, but no one wanted the job. The fourth officer finally went, quickly came back, and didn't say much beyond what the reporters had already told.

After this, Blake's diary became more fearful and nervous. He blamed himself for not doing something sooner and worried about what might happen if the power went out again. During thunderstorms, he even called the electric company several times, begging them to prevent another blackout. His notes also showed he was troubled by the missing items—the box, the stone, and the skeleton. He assumed someone, or something, had taken them, but he didn't know who or how.

Blake's biggest fear, though, was the strange connection he felt growing between himself and whatever he had disturbed in that dark steeple. He believed the creature somehow knew him now. Friends who visited him said he often sat staring out the window at the faraway tower, lost in thought. His diary mentioned the same nightmare over and over and a deepening bond between him and the thing in his sleep. He even wrote about waking up one night, fully dressed and walking outside, headed toward the west, without knowing why. Over and over, he wrote that the thing knew where to find him.

The week after July 30 was when Blake really started falling apart. He stayed in bed, ordered food by phone, and tied cords around his ankles every night to stop himself from sleepwalking. He told people it was the only way to keep himself in bed.

In his diary, Blake described a terrible experience that caused his breakdown. One night, after going to bed, he suddenly found himself in almost complete darkness. All he could see were faint bluish lines of light. The air was filled with a horrible smell, and he could hear soft, creepy noises above him. Every time he moved, he bumped into something on the floor. And each time, he heard a faint reply from above—a slow sliding sound, like wood scraping against wood.

While feeling his way through the darkness, Blake's hands touched a stone pillar with a flat top. Later, he found a ladder built into the wall and slowly climbed it, heading toward an area with a stronger smell and a hot, burning wind blowing down on him. As he moved, strange and shifting images filled his mind—visions of robed, hooded figures that didn't look human, endless deserts with tall, carved stones reaching into the sky, underwater towers and walls, and swirling spaces filled with black mist and faint purple glows. He imagined a huge, endless black void where stars and planets spun in even darker space. In the center, he pictured the ancient god Azathoth, blind and mindless, surrounded by dancing shapes and the constant, eerie sound of a flute played by something unnamable.

Then, a loud noise from the outside world snapped him out of his daze and made him realize how horrible his situation was. He never knew what the sound was— maybe it was a leftover firework from one of the many summer celebrations on Federal Hill. But it scared him so badly that he screamed, let go of the ladder, and stumbled blindly across the dark room.

Suddenly he knew where he was and rushed down the tight spiral staircase, hurting himself as he fell and hit things along the way. He ran through the huge, dusty church nave, through the shadowy basement, out into the rainy night, and down the creepy hill full of old buildings. He dashed across the quiet city and back up to his house on the east side.

When he woke the next morning, he was lying on the floor of his study, still fully dressed. He was covered in dust and cobwebs, sore all over, and when he looked in the mirror, he saw his hair was singed. His clothes still held a strange, awful smell. That's when his nerves finally broke. From then on, he stayed in his robe, too exhausted to do much besides stare out his west window, flinch at thunder, and scribble frantic thoughts into his diary.

The big storm hit just before midnight on August 8. Lightning flashed all over the city, and there were even two unusual fireballs reported. The rain poured down, and the thunder was so loud that hardly anyone could sleep. Blake was panicking about the power going out and even called the electric company around 1 a.m., but the phone lines had already been shut down for safety. He kept writing in his diary with messy, panicked handwriting, even in the dark.

He kept the house dark so he could see out his window better, watching the city's rooftops and the faraway lights of Federal Hill. From time to time, he'd write quick, nervous notes in the diary—phrases like "The lights must not go," "It knows where I am," "I must destroy it," and "It is calling to me, but maybe it won't hurt me this time."

Then, the lights in the city went out. According to the power company, this happened at 2:12 a.m. Blake didn't write the time in his diary—just a single line: "Lights out—God help me." On Federal Hill, people were just as scared. Groups of men were out in the rain with candles, flashlights, oil lamps, crucifixes, and lucky charms from southern Italy. They cheered when lightning flashed and made protective hand signs whenever the storm quieted down. The wind grew stronger and blew out most of the candles, making things even darker. Someone went to wake up Father Merluzzo from Spirito Santo Church, and he came to the square to say prayers. Strange sounds were clearly coming from the dark tower.

At 2:35 a.m., several witnesses reported what happened next. These included Father Merluzzo, Officer William J. Monahan, and nearly eighty men who were near the church. Nothing they saw could be proved to be supernatural, but there were lots of theories—strange gases from the old, rotting building, maybe some chemical reaction, or even someone faking the whole thing. Still, what happened took less than three minutes, and Father Merluzzo kept checking his watch.

It started with louder thumping noises from inside the tower. A terrible smell, worse than before, poured out of the church. Then something heavy crashed down outside—the wooden slats from one of the tower's east windows. Right after that, the smell became overpowering. People near the church felt sick, and many nearly fainted. The air shook with a sound like giant wings flapping, and a strong wind tore through the crowd, ripping off hats and flipping umbrellas. No one could see much in the darkness, but some said they saw a big, shapeless shadow move across the sky like a fast-moving cloud.

That was it. Everyone was frozen with fear, unsure of what they had just witnessed. They stayed in place, and a few moments later, they prayed when lightning lit up the sky again, followed by a deafening thunderclap. The rain stopped about thirty minutes later, and fifteen minutes after that, the city lights came back on. Relieved, the tired and soaked crowd slowly went home.

The newspapers barely mentioned the event, including it as part of the overall storm coverage. But they did say that the strange light and loud sound had been even stronger to the east, where people also noticed the same awful smell. On College Hill, the explosion had woken up everyone, and people were confused and scared. Some said they saw a strange flash of light at the top of the hill and felt a sudden gust of wind that stripped leaves off trees and damaged gardens. People guessed lightning had struck somewhere nearby, but no sign of a lightning strike was ever found. One student thought he saw a dark, ugly cloud just before the flash, but no one else could confirm it. Still, everyone agreed that a strong wind from the west and a horrible smell had come right before the lightning, followed by a burnt odor that lingered afterward.

These details were looked at closely because they might be connected to how Robert Blake died. Students living in the Psi Delta house, whose back windows faced Blake's study, noticed something strange on the morning of the 9th. They saw his pale face in the west-facing window and thought something was off about his expression. When they saw the same face in the same place that evening, they got worried. They waited to see if the lights in his apartment would come on.

When they didn't, they rang his doorbell. Eventually, they had a police officer break down the door.

Blake's stiff body was still sitting straight at his desk by the window. When the people entered and saw his wide, bulging eyes and the terrified look frozen on his face, they turned away in shock and disgust. The coroner later checked the body and said Blake had died from an electrical shock or stress caused by a nearby electrical burst. He didn't focus on the horrible expression, saying it could have come from the intense fear of someone with a wild imagination. He got that idea from the books, paintings, and handwritten pages in the apartment, along with the scribbled diary found on the desk. Blake had kept writing until the very end. The pencil with a broken tip was still clenched tightly in his hand.

The last diary entries, written after the power went out, were messy and hard to read. Some people who studied them came up with very different ideas from the official report. Still, most didn't believe these other theories. One man, a superstitious doctor named Dexter, only made things seem weirder by throwing the strange box and glowing stone into the deepest part of Narragansett Bay. That stone had been found glowing inside the dark tower. Most people believe Blake simply had an overactive imagination, worsened by the dark history he had uncovered.

Here is what could be made out from the last pages of Blake's diary:

"Lights still off—it must've been five minutes. Everything depends on the lightning. I hope it keeps going!... Something is breaking through it.... The rain, thunder, and wind are too loud.... Something is trying to take over my mind....

"I'm having memory problems. I'm seeing things I never knew before. Other worlds, other galaxies.... It's dark.... But the lightning seems dark and the darkness seems bright....

"This can't be the real hill and church I'm seeing in total darkness. It must be my eyes playing tricks from the lightning flashes. I hope the Italians are out there with candles if the lightning stops!

"What am I afraid of? Isn't it just an appearance of Nyarlathotep, who once appeared as a man in ancient Egypt? I remember Yuggoth, and the far-off world of Shaggai, and the endless blackness of dead planets....

"That long flight through space ... it can't pass through the universe of light ... shaped by thoughts trapped in the Shining Trapezohedron ... pushed through glowing, terrible space....

"My name is Blake—Robert Harrison Blake of 620 East Knapp Street, Milwaukee, Wisconsin.... I am still on this planet....

"Azathoth, have mercy!—there's no more lightning—this is awful—I can see everything now, but not with my eyes—it's a strange kind of vision—light feels like darkness and darkness feels like light... those people on the hill... guarding... candles and charms... their priests...

"I can't tell how far things are—everything feels both near and far. There's no light—no glass—I can see the steeple, that tower, that window—I can hear—Roderick Usher—I'm losing my mind or already lost it—that thing is moving and reaching around in the tower—I am it, and it is me—I want to escape... I must escape and merge the powers.... It knows where I am....

"I am Robert Blake, but I see the tower in the dark. There's a horrible smell... my senses feel all twisted... the boards on that tower window are breaking apart.... Iä... ngai... ygg....

"I see it—it's coming—it's like a wind from hell—a massive blur—black wings—Yog-Sothoth, help me—the three-lobed burning eye...."

# Thank You for Reading

Dear Reader,

We hope this timeless classic has sparked your imagination and enriched your literary journey. Now that you've turned the final page, we want to share a vision for the future of reading—one where every classic you've ever wanted to explore is at your fingertips, in a format that best suits your life.

We'd like to invite you to gain immediate, unlimited digital & audiobook access to hundreds of the most treasured literary classics ever written—along with the option to secure deluxe paperback, hardcover & box set editions at printing cost. Together, we can spark a new global literary renaissance alongside our small, independent publishing house called "The Library of Alexandria."

Thousands of years ago, the Library of Alexandria stood as a beacon of knowledge—until it was lost to history. We aim to reignite that spirit of preservation and discovery right now, in the modern age—only this time, it's accessible to all, in every language and every format.

Picture a world where every timeless classic, novel, poem, or philosophical treatise is not only available to read but also updated for today's readers—modernized, translated into any language or dialect, and ready to enjoy in any format you choose, whether that is in an eBook, audiobook, paperback, or deluxe hardcover & box set version a printing cost.

By joining our movement to rebuild the modern Library of Alexandria, you become part of an unprecedented mission to offer:

- **Unlimited Audiobook & eBook Access to the Greatest Classics of All Time**

  Instantly explore thousands of legendary works, from Plato and Shakespeare to Jane Austen and Leo Tolstoy. All are instantly ready to read or listen to, giving you a complete literary universe at your fingertips.

- **Paperback & Deluxe Editions at Printing Costs:**

  Purchase any title in a paperback, deluxe hardbound, or deluxe boxset edition at printing costs, shipped right to your doorstep. Curate your personal library of Alexandria with editions worthy of display— crafted to last, designed to captivate, and delivered straight to your door.

- **Modern translations for Contemporary Readers in all languages and dialects**

  Discover a vast selection of classics reimagined in clear, current language—no more struggling with outdated phrases or obscure references. Next to the original versions, we aim to offer translations in as many languages and dialects as possible.

  As we continue our translation efforts and add new languages, readers everywhere can connect with these works as if they were written today. By bridging linguistic divides, you're contributing to ensuring that these timeless stories become more meaningful, accessible, and inspiring for people across the globe.

- **Your Personal Library of Alexandria:**

  Over the months and years, you'll curate a unique physical archive of classics—each volume a testament to your taste, curiosity, and love of knowledge. It's not just about owning books—it's about curating a cultural legacy you'll cherish and pass down for generations to come.

- **Join a Global Literary Renaissance:**

  Your support fuels an ongoing mission: allowing us to reinvest in offering deluxe print editions (including special boxsets) at their true cost, broaden the range of available formats and translations, and extend the reach of these works to new audiences worldwide. By joining today, you're not just preserving a legacy of masterpieces; you set in motion a powerful wave of literary accessibility.

We are more than a publisher—we're a movement, and we can't do it alone. Your support lets us scale our mission, preserving and reimagining history's greatest works for tomorrow's readers.

**Become a Torchbearer of knowledge.**

Thank you for picking up this book and allowing us into your literary journey. As you turn the pages, know that you're part of something larger: a global effort to keep these stories alive, share their wisdom across borders and generations, and spark a true cultural revival for the modern era.

If this resonates with you—please consider taking the next step by visiting:

**www.libraryofalexandria.com**

With gratitude and a shared love of knowledge,

The Modern Library of Alexandria Team

Visit:

www.libraryofalexandria.com

Or scan the code below: